Scaredy Dog

by Stephen Lemberg

pictures by Cat Bowman Smith

AN UMBRELLA BOOK

Alfred A. Knopf • New York

AN UMBRELLA BOOK PUBLISHED BY ALFRED A. KNOPF, INC.

Library of Congress Cataloging-in-Publication Data
Lemberg, Stephen H.
Scaredy dog / by Stephen Lemberg ; illustrated by Cat Bowman Smith.
p.   cm.
"An Umbrella book."
Summary: Rufus, a dog who is afraid of everything, saves the day
when his owner is in danger.
ISBN 0-679-83175-4 (trade) — ISBN 0-679-93175-9 (lib. bdg.)
[1. Dogs—Fiction. 2. Fear—Fiction.] I. Smith, Cat Bowman,
ill. II. Title.
PZ7.L53735Sc   1994
[E]—dc20   92-24440

Manufactured in the United States of America
2 4 6 8 0 9 7 5 3 1

With special thanks to Stephanie Spinner, this story is
dedicated to Barbara and our four original scaredy dogs
—S. L.

Dedicated to Wanda Webster, helper of critters
—C. B. S.

On a small green island in the middle of a bright blue bay lived a child who had a puppy named Rufus. Rufus had long floppy ears and a little black nose, and when he was happy, he would stick out his tongue and go, "*Ha-ah-ha-ah-ha-ah-ha-ah-ha*."

Every summer morning, the child and the puppy ran across a flower-filled meadow to Carol's store to buy a newspaper. And every summer morning, Rufus carried the newspaper home in his mouth while the child picked a bouquet of wildflowers.

Every summer afternoon, the child and Rufus walked
down the path to the beach. And there, beside the bright
blue bay, the child threw a red ball to Rufus, who would
bring it back, again and again and again.

Every summer evening, the child brushed and scrubbed and washed behind the ears. Rufus sat on the floor watching, with his tongue hanging out, going, "*Ha-ah-ha-ah-ha-ah-ha-ah-ha.*"

One summer morning, the child and Rufus were running across the flower-filled meadow when a big yellow butterfly came fluttering along.

"*Wee-wee-wee,*" cried Rufus, stopping in his tracks.

"*Wee-wee-wee,*" he cried, and he started to run the other way.

"Wait, Rufus!" ordered the child. "Are you afraid of a butterfly? You are such a scaredy dog!"

"That butterfly won't hurt you. It just wants to say good morning," said the child, patting Rufus on his furry little head. "You silly scaredy dog."

"*Ruff, ruff, ruff,*" barked Rufus. To show that he was not afraid of butterflies anymore, he barked, "*Ruff, ruff, ruff.*"

That afternoon the child and Rufus were walking down the
path to the beach when a little brown rabbit darted out of the
honeysuckle and sat down right in front of the puppy.

"*Wee-wee-wee*," cried Rufus, stopping in his tracks.
"*Wee-wee-wee*," he cried, and he started to run the
other way.

"Wait, Rufus!" cried the child. "Are you afraid of a
bunny rabbit? You are such a scaredy dog!

"Dogs are supposed to chase rabbits, not run away from
them," said the child, scratching Rufus between his long
floppy ears. "You silly scaredy dog."

"*Ruff, ruff, ruff,*" barked Rufus. To show that he was not afraid of bunny rabbits anymore, he barked, "*Ruff, ruff, ruff,*" and the little brown rabbit hopped quickly away.

That evening, before going to bed, the child was brushing and scrubbing and washing behind the ears while Rufus sat on the floor watching, with his tongue hanging out, going, "*Ha-ah-ha-ah-ha-ah-ha-ah-ha.*"

Outside, a full moon was shining and the crickets were chirping.

"*Rrrickitt, rrrickitt, rrrickitt,*" chirped the crickets.

Suddenly, a cricket came hopping through the window and landed on the floor.

"*Wee-wee-wee*," cried Rufus, jumping straight up in the air.
"*Wee-wee-wee*," he cried, and started to run away.
"Where are you going, Rufus?" cried the child. "Are you
afraid of that teeny tiny cricket? You are such a scaredy dog."

"That cricket won't hurt you. It just wants to play you a cricket song," said the child, rubbing Rufus on his pink tummy. "You silly scaredy dog."

"*Ruff, ruff, ruff,*" barked Rufus. To show that he was not afraid of crickets anymore, he barked, "*Ruff, ruff, ruff.*"

The very next day, the child and Rufus were playing on the beach. The child was throwing the red ball to Rufus when a mother swan and her four baby swans, called cygnets, came swimming by.

"*Wee-wee-wee,*" cried Rufus, and he stopped chasing the ball.

"*Wee-wee-wee,*" he cried, and started running the other way.

"Wait, Rufus!" ordered the child. "Are you afraid of
swans? I am tired of you being such a scaredy dog."

"Swans are pretty. They will not hurt you. I am not afraid of swans," bragged the child. "Just watch me and I will show you how silly you are!" And with that the child walked to the edge of the bay and reached toward one of the little cygnets.

"*Hisssss!*" said the mother swan, flapping her gigantic wings. "*Hisssss!*" she cried, rushing over the water toward the child.

"Help! Help!" called the child, who was suddenly very scared indeed.

The angry mother swan came even closer, hissing and snapping and nipping at the frightened child.

Then, "*Ruff, ruff, ruff,*" barked Rufus in his fiercest voice, running toward the mother swan. "*Grrrrr, grrrrr, grrrrr,*" he growled, protecting his friend.

The mother swan turned away from the child and
snapped at Rufus. "*Hissss,*" she threatened. "*Hissss!*"
Then, stretching her long, long neck, she grabbed her
baby in her bill and swam away.

The child ran back up the beach, but Rufus stood at the very edge of the bay, barking, "*Ruff, ruff, ruff,*" until the swan and her four cygnets had paddled out of sight. Then he turned and proudly pranced up to the child.

"Rufus!" said the child. "You saved me from that terrible swan! I love you and I will never call you 'scaredy dog' again."

Rufus was so happy that the child was proud of him that
he stuck out his tongue and went, "*Ha-ah-ha-ah-ha-ah-ha-
ah-ha,*" all the way home.